Lizzie McGuire

The IMPORTANCE OF BEING GORDO

Adapted by Jasmine Jones
Based on the series created by Terri Minsky
Part One is based on a teleplay written
by Douglas Tuber & Tim Maile.
Part Two is based on a teleplay written
by Kris Lowe.

Watch it on
DISNEY CHANNEL
abc Kids

DISNEY PRESS

VOLO

New York

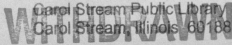

Printed in the United States of America

First Edition
1 3 5 7 9 10 8 6 4 2

Library of Congress Catalog Card Number on file.

ISBN 0-7868-4656-9
For more Disney Press fun, visit www.disneybooks.com
Visit DisneyChannel.com

PART
ONE

CHAPTER ONE

"I was watching this spy movie last night," Lizzie McGuire's best friend David "Gordo" Gordon said as he followed Lizzie and her other best friend, Miranda Sanchez, into the McGuires' hallway. "And it got me thinking—why do supervillains always want to take over the world?"

Lizzie thought for a minute. That was the thing about Gordo—you could always count on him to come up with a random question that was actually a pretty good, if not weird, point. "Well," Lizzie said, "I think it would be kind of cool to rule the world." She smiled at Miranda. "I mean, you could meet any celebrity you wanted."

Actually, Lizzie thought, there could be a lot of fringe benefits.

i could pass a new law making Ethan Craft worship me.

If ever there were a reason to take over the world, Ethan Craft was *so* it. Ethan was in Lizzie's grade at Hillridge Junior High, and both she and Miranda agreed that he was like dry ice—totally cool and totally hot at the same time. Hanging with him would be the cornerstone of Lizzie's reign as Imperial Empress of Planet Earth!

Gordo shook his head. "You'd have to be in charge of *everything*," he pointed out, gesturing wildly. "What if the electricity went out in Stockholm? Or there's a mud slide in Argentina? Or Thailand's being infested with aphids—I mean, what do you do?"

Lizzie furrowed her brow. "I never thought of it that way, Gordo," she admitted. Sheesh, I had enough trouble picking out this bandanna this morning, Lizzie thought as she flipped the ends of her pink sparkly head scarf over her shoulders. I would totally not want to have to add "Deal with Thailand aphids" to my To Do list.

"Well, luckily, I don't want to rule the world," Miranda said with a grin as she folded her arms across her chest. "I want to be a singer on a cruise ship."

Lizzie smiled dubiously at her friend, who was wearing a typical-Miranda funky outfit— dark red streaks in her jet-black hair, sideways sun visor, black pants, red shirt that read "Love," and chunky black shoes. Right, Lizzie thought, I can just see Miranda in some gold lamé dress singing "Love Will Keep Us Together" for the shuffleboard set. Give me the aphids any day.

"Hey, kids," Mrs. McGuire said as she walked into the kitchen with an enormous box covered in pastel wrapping paper. "Lizzie—you got a package from Gammy McGuire," Lizzie's mom said, as she handed the box over to her daughter.

"Excellent," Lizzie said with little excitement.

"My grandmother can't remember when my birthday is," she explained to her best friends, rolling her eyes, "so she just sends me stuff every couple months, just to make sure." Of course, the stuff is always lame, Lizzie thought. Once she sent me a sweater with a unicorn on it that was so ugly it nearly ruined my life.

She ripped open the box.

"Ooh, maybe it's that scarf you want!" Miranda said eagerly. "Or those cool rhinestone sunglasses! Or that jewelry box!"

Lizzie pulled the gift out of the box. Her grandmother had sent her a board game. "'Dwarflord: The Conquest,'" Lizzie read aloud. She was not impressed.

Miranda grimaced, as though she had caught a whiff of something foul. "Or it could, you know, *reek*."

"'The game of dragon monarchs and dwarf warriors,'" Lizzie went on, reading from the lid of the game. She sighed. Gammy's gifts just get worse and worse, she thought.

"Like I said . . ." Miranda put in.

Lizzie kept reading as she headed into the kitchen. "'Imagine you're an exiled Dwarflord, seeking to reclaim your kingdom, stolen by an evil wizard and guarded by his dragon slaves.'"

Imagine you're an exiled board game, doomed to become one with a landfill, Lizzie thought as she lifted the trash can lid.

"Hey!" Lizzie's mother gave her a disapproving frown as she grabbed the game out of Lizzie's hand. "You're not throwing your gift away."

Gordo looked at Mrs. McGuire as though she were crazy. "Why not?" Gordo demanded. "Didn't you hear about the Dwarflords?"

Mrs. McGuire looked at the ceiling in frustration. "I want you to play it at least one time," she said to Lizzie, "and then, if you don't like it, we're going to donate it to charity."

Lizzie sighed. Donate it to charity? she thought. Haven't those poor children suffered enough? But she knew that there was no point in arguing with her mother.

"Fine, I'll play it." Lizzie turned to her friends. "C'mon, Gordo, Miranda, let's get this over with."

"Oh," Miranda said quickly, pursing her lips, "I gotta go home and clean fish." She pointed at the door. "See, my dad went fishing, so I have to go home and . . ." Miranda raised her eyebrows, obviously trying to think of something that would clinch her excuse. ". . . gut them."

Lizzie narrowed her eyes. And I thought that *I* was a lousy liar, she said to herself, watching her friend squirm. Lizzie looked at Gordo.

"Yeah, and I'm going to go home and try to

grow a mustache," Gordo threw in quickly. "I've been meaning to."

"Miranda, I let you borrow my blue top, and you got deviled eggs all over it, okay?" Lizzie snapped. "You owe me."

"All right, all right . . ." Miranda grumbled.

"And Gordo, if you don't play, I'll tell everyone what you did at Dakota Himmelfarb's Fourth of July party," Lizzie said, lifting her eyes knowingly.

Gordo looked blank.

"You know," Lizzie prompted, "with the mustard—"

"Hey, what are we wasting time yakking for?" Gordo said quickly. "Let's play Dwarflord!"

Lizzie nodded. She hated to stoop to blackmail, but if it was the only way to get Gordo to play Dwarflord, she guessed she had to go with it. Besides, I'm glad I finally got to use "the mustard incident" to my benefit, she thought. Although it was really gross.

Still, it wasn't half as gross as Dwarflord.

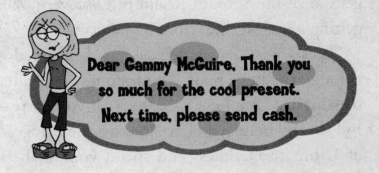

Dear Gammy McGuire, Thank you so much for the cool present. Next time, please send cash.

* * *

"Okay, Lizzie." Miranda scanned the rule book. At least, I think it's the rule book, Lizzie thought as she gaped at the huge tome. It's so thick, it looks like it could be the Los Angeles phone book. The game board was spread out before them, covered in playing pieces. This game may not be fun, Lizzie thought, but it sure is complicated. "You're in the Seventh Realm of Discovery, so you have to roll the

Dream Dice, and the toe-bone of Rumblepeter Goblin-beater," Miranda explained.

Lizzie rolled her eyes. "But I thought I could get out of the Seventh Realm of Discovery by getting a wish-feather from a mooncat."

"Let's see . . ." Miranda said as she flipped through the huge book. "Lodestones . . . troll blessings . . . oh, here it is. It says if you don't roll the toe-bone, you have to cross the Bridge of Ultimate Darkness and spend your wish-feather on Insanity Syrup." Miranda looked up, completely confused.

I think I already drank some Insanity Syrup, Lizzie thought miserably. That's the only logical reason I would be playing this game.

Whatever happened to hide-and-go-seek? Simple game—you count to fifty, I go hide. Ideally with Ethan Craft. On a yacht.

"We've been playing this game for twenty minutes now, okay?" Lizzie said impatiently. "Gammy McGuire's gift has been . . ." Lizzie searched for the right word. ". . . enjoyed."

Miranda nodded.

"You guys just want to quit 'cause I'm winning," Gordo said.

Miranda gaped at him. "You are?" she said as she stared down at the rule book and flipped through the pages. "How can you tell?"

Gordo shrugged. "Well, I've acquired The Thirteen Skulls," he said with a grin, ". . . and you know what *that* means."

"No, I really don't," Lizzie told him, shaking her head. "Nor do I care."

Is Gordo serious? Lizzie wondered. I'm sitting here thinking that Dwarflord puts the bore in board game, and he's talking magic skulls?

"Well, I can trade them in for a Shape-shifting Button," Gordo explained. "I turn into the Dragon Monarch—then I need to get an Inferno Robe and a Smoke Shield."

Miranda looked over at Lizzie. "Mall?" she suggested.

"You bet." Lizzie nodded and hauled herself out of her chair.

Lizzie and Miranda headed for the door.

"All right, all right—" Gordo surrendered. "I'll come."

"Bye, Mom," Lizzie called as she and her friends headed out, passing her annoying little brother, Matt. "Bye, Dad," Lizzie said, ignoring Matt.

"Bye, honey," Mr. McGuire said.

"Bye," Lizzie's mom chimed in.

"Mom, Dad," Matt said as he walked into the living room where his parents were sitting on the couch. "I need a ride to the docks."

"How come, Champ?" Mr. McGuire asked.

"To check out some wharf rats."

"Are you talking about colorful waterfront characters named Cap'n Salty," Mrs. McGuire asked hopefully, "or are you talking about actual disease-carrying rodents?"

"The disease-carrying rodents," Matt confirmed. "I'm studying wildlife for school," he added brightly, rubbing his hands together.

Mrs. McGuire's expression darkened. "Well, you are not studying rats, young man."

"Okay," Matt said, dropping his arms in disappointment. Then, suddenly, his face brightened again. "Well, I'm going to go ride my bike up into the hills to check out the rattlesnake nests." He turned and headed for the door. "See you at dinner."

"Come here, Indiana Jones," Mrs. McGuire commanded. "You can study nature right here at home."

"But there isn't any here," Matt griped. "Dad killed all the fire ants with spray, trapped all the mice, and hosed away all the wasps' nests."

Mrs. McGuire's mouth dropped open in shock. "Sam," she said, accusingly, "how could you?"

"What—" Mr. McGuire said defensively, "you *want* fire ants?" He shook his head. His wife had bothered him for three weeks to do something about the ants. But she had never mentioned that she expected her husband to use nonviolence to persuade them to live elsewhere.

Mr. McGuire suddenly looked like he had an idea. "Hey, there's a bird's nest in the oak tree in the backyard."

Mrs. McGuire rolled her eyes. "Go quick," she said to Matt, gesturing toward the backyard, "go study before your dad cuts the tree down."

"Good idea," Matt said, nodding knowingly. "I bet he's just itching to chop that puppy down."

Mr. McGuire sighed. There was just no way to win.

CHAPTER TWO

"**S**o—Digital Bean after school?" Miranda suggested to her two best friends as they sat at their usual lunch table. The Digital Bean cybercafe was their favorite hangout, and Lizzie was sure everyone would be up for it.

"No." Gordo shook his head. "I can't make it."

Lizzie frowned. Gordo always loved hanging out at the Bean—he claimed that their smoothies were the highlight of his day. Lizzie guessed he must have a good reason for skipping. "Why?" she asked. "What are you doing?"

"Playing Dwarflord," Gordo said.

Lizzie cracked up. That was a good one, she thought. He'd actually managed to say it with a straight face and everything. "No, really— what are you doing?"

"I'm playing Dwarflord," Gordo repeated. Like he was serious.

And that was when Lizzie realized—he *was* serious. "Why on earth would you want to do that?" Lizzie demanded.

"Because I liked it," Gordo said simply. "And it turns out that there's a Dwarf Tribe right here on campus."

"Really?" Miranda asked. "Do they get, like, special parking or anything?"

Lizzie punched her friend in the arm. Miranda could be so rude sometimes.

"A Dwarf Tribe is what you call a group of people who get together and play the game on a regular basis," Gordo explained.

Lizzie gave Gordo a dubious look. "I thought the name for that was—" She lifted her finger to her lips. *"Buh-buh-buh-buh."*

"You just don't understand it," Gordo said patiently. "It's more of a guy's game—the epic struggle of good versus evil, the intricate strategies, the mighty deeds of fearsome warriors."

Lizzie looked at Gordo. Fearsome warriors? she thought.

"Hail, Gordo Glimmerfoe!" Larry Tudgeman called as he strode over to Lizzie's table. Larry was pretty much the mighty leader of the Hillridge nerds, and right now, a whole troop of his dorkalicious friends stood behind him—and they were all decked out in brown cloaks and rope belts. Talk about the quickest way to top the Fashion Don't list! Some of them were even carrying spears and shields. "The Tribe salutes its newest questling!" Larry finished.

The tribe placed their fists on their hearts and then on their foreheads, then thrust them into the air and shouted, "Huzzah!"

So this must be the Dork Tribe—I mean, Dwarf Tribe, Lizzie thought.

Miranda peered doubtfully at Gordo and his Tribe. "Farewell and good luck, Gordo Hammertoe," she said sarcastically.

"Yeah, have fun storming the castle," Lizzie added.

"A thousand thanks, maidens fair," Larry said, sweeping into a low, courtly bow.

"You know," Gordo whispered as he stood up next to Larry, "they're making fun of us."

Larry's eyes grew wide in disbelief. "They are?" He scowled. "Fine." Staring at Lizzie and Miranda intensely, Larry held his arms in front of him, gesticulated in a series of intricate waves, then shot his hands toward Miranda and Lizzie, fingers wiggling.

Did he just put a hex on us? Lizzie wondered. Or was he practicing his water-ballet routine?

Larry nodded in satisfaction. "That ought to show 'em," he said, turning back to the tribe.

The tribe pounded their hearts and heads in agreement. "Huzzah." The brown-cloaked nerds trekked off, with Gordo trailing behind.

Lizzie stared at Miranda. "What *was* that?"

But Miranda didn't have an answer. Whatever it was, Lizzie decided, it was definitely freaky.

CHAPTER THREE

Matt shifted his position. The branch wasn't the most comfortable seat he'd ever had in his life, but his father had insisted that they climb the tree to look at the bird's eggs. And Matt had to admit that they did have a good view of the eggs. Not that they were doing anything.

"This is boring," Matt said.

"No, it isn't," Mr. McGuire protested. He pointed toward the eggs, which continued to do about as much as the eggs in the refrigerator. "This is the whole miracle of nature at work. This is life renewing itself."

Matt yawned.

Mr. McGuire didn't give up. "This is the universe unfolding according to a grand plan."

"And it's boring," Matt added. He stared at the eggs some more, wishing that this "miracle of nature" involved something exciting, like the eggs of the deadly and now-extinct velociraptor, instead of these stupid bird eggs that didn't do anything.

"Hey, mighty bird-watchers," Mrs. McGuire called from the foot of the tree, "I brought you some snacks." She held up a couple of juice boxes and protein bars.

"Oh, great," Matt said quickly, "I'll come right down and get 'em."

"That's okay," Mrs. McGuire said brightly,

eager to support both Matt's nature project and the father-son time that was keeping the house so quiet, "you don't have to. I can toss it up to you."

"No, no, no—that's way too dangerous," Matt insisted, clearly looking for an excuse to ditch his dad. "I'll come right down."

Matt scrambled down the tree as though it were on fire. He grabbed a box of juice and a protein bar and scurried toward the rear deck.

"Hey, where are you going, sweetie?" Mrs. McGuire called.

"Um . . . bathroom," Matt lied. He turned toward the house and hurried inside.

Mr. McGuire looked down at the top of his wife's head and asked, "He's not coming back, is he?"

"I wouldn't count on it. Here's your juice," Mrs. McGuire said. She tossed the box drink into the tree, but it bounced off her husband's head and plummeted back to the ground. It occurred to Mrs. McGuire that her son might have had a point about the danger of tossing snacks into trees.

"Anybody home?" a voice called out as Mrs. McGuire bent over to pick up the juice.

It was Miranda's father, and he was carrying a hedge trimmer.

"Hey, Sam," Mrs. McGuire called up to her husband, "Edward Sanchez is here."

"Oooh!" Mr. McGuire groaned. He didn't want to take his eyes off of the eggs for a second—who knew when they might hatch?—but now he'd have to climb out of the tree and talk "hedges" with Miranda's dad.

"He's standing right next to me," Mrs. McGuire clarified.

"Oooh!" Mr. McGuire said, pretending to be delighted. "Hey, Eduardo," he said uncomfortably, "remember that fifteen bucks I borrowed from you? I just keep forgetting to give it back."

"Oh, forget about that," Mr. Sanchez said, waving his hand. "I have."

Mr. McGuire grinned. "Oooh!"

"I brought back Sam's hedge trimmer," Mr. Sanchez said to Lizzie's mom, holding up the oversized shears. "My topiary is turning out well. What's Sam doing in the tree?"

"Oh, it's a school project for Matt," Mrs. McGuire explained.

Mr. Sanchez nodded knowingly.

"In fact," Mrs. McGuire went on, "would you get these up to him?" She handed the box of juice and the protein bar to Mr. Sanchez. "I'm afraid he's going to die of thirst."

"Oh, sure," Mr. Sanchez said, dropping the hedge trimmers on the ground at the foot of the tree. Then he turned toward the trunk and started up. "I'm coming right up, Sam."

"Righty-o," Mr. McGuire called from amid the leaves. "Thanks," he said as Mr. Sanchez handed over the snacks.

Mr. Sanchez caught sight of the eggs. "Oh, a bird's nest," he said.

"Yeah, a sparrow's, I think," Lizzie's dad replied as he punched a straw into the box of juice. "Hey, you want some protein bar?"

"Oh, thanks," Mr. Sanchez said, staring at the eggs. "Wait, don't hog all the juice!"

"Sorry," Mr. McGuire apologized as he handed over the apple juice. "Only let me have some of that protein bar."

Mr. Sanchez reluctantly handed it over.

Meanwhile, upstairs, Lizzie was having some trouble with a school assignment of her own. So she picked up her trusty phone and gave her best friend a ring.

"Hello?" Miranda said as she answered the

phone while running her vacuum across the floor of her room.

"Hey, do you understand this English homework?" Lizzie asked. She was vacuuming, too. Talking on the phone while doing chores was part of the friends' new "time-maximization" plan, which was all about multitasking.

"I understand that it's a pain in the rear," Miranda griped, pushing her vacuum across the floor. "I guess we could go down to the library and check out some reference books. Or we could—"

"Call Gordo," Lizzie finished for her. Gordo was *way* faster than the library—and about twice as reliable. She pressed the flash button and called Gordo using her ever-handy three-way calling.

"Huzzah!" Lizzie heard a crowd cheer in the background as Gordo picked up the phone. "Gordo," he said into the receiver.

What was *that*? Lizzie wondered. But she decided not to get into it. "Explain prepositional phrases," she said.

"Sorry, I'm kind of busy right now," Gordo said sheepishly.

"This is your homework hour!" Miranda said in a shocked tone that could hardly be heard over her vacuum cleaner. "What are you doing?" she asked, wondering what could be more important to Gordo than homework.

"Nothing special," Gordo hedged.

Now Lizzie could hear people chanting in Gordo's room. "The hour of magic is upon us! The hour of magic is upon us!" Was that Larry Tudgeman's voice? Lizzie wondered. "Are you playing that munchkin game again?" she demanded. Please, tell me that Gordo isn't wearing some brown burlap robe and a rope belt, she begged silently.

"Yeah," Gordo snapped. "And I'm about to vanquish the Winged Werewolf to the Eighth Vortex, so I can't really help you with your prepositions right now."

Over on Gordo's end of the line, Larry asked, "Is that Lizzie and Miranda?"

Gordo nodded, and Larry scowled. He waved his hands and aimed another "spell" at the receiver in Gordo's hand.

At the other end of the line, Lizzie's and Miranda's vacuums suddenly fell silent. Lizzie frowned. Dumb vacuum, she thought, checking the plug. Then she realized Miranda's vacuum had gone silent, too! Bizarre-o!

"Look, I have got to roll the toe-bone," Gordo said. "I'll see you guys later." He clicked off.

Miranda shook her silent vacuum, wondering what had gone wrong. Then she decided to forget about it and focus her attention on the real problem at hand. "I'm a little worried about this," she said.

"Me, too," Lizzie admitted. "You know how Gordo obsesses about things."

"I mean, I'm worried about how we're going to get this homework done," Miranda clarified. "My mom's working tonight. And my dad's up in a tree with your dad."

"Well, I'm worried about Gordo," Lizzie countered. "He's way too interested in this game. And Tudgeman plays it. That puts up a red flag right there."

"He's going to lose interest in it eventually," Miranda said. "Just like his carrier pigeons."

Lizzie thought about that. It was true— Gordo used to spend hours with those birds. What happened to those pigeons, again? Lizzie wondered. Oh, yeah . . .

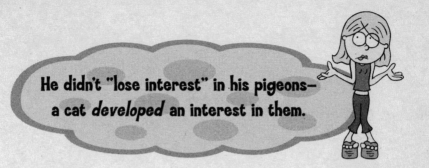

He didn't "lose interest" in his pigeons—
a cat *developed* an interest in them.

Lizzie heaved a sigh. "I hope you're right," she said into the phone. "But I'm gonna keep an eye on him."

And I'm going to keep another eye on my prepositions, Lizzie told herself, as soon as I figure out what the heck is wrong with this vacuum.

CHAPTER FOUR

"So, are we going to study together?" Lizzie asked hopefully as she walked down the school stairs with her two best friends.

Gordo shook his head. He was staring at a piece of paper, barely paying attention to anything Lizzie was saying. "I can't," he said absently. "I've got other plans."

Lizzie peered at the piece of paper. It was covered in strange markings. Don't tell me these "other plans" involve dwarves from the Eighth Dimension, she thought.

Just then, Veruca, captain of the Mathletes and one of Larry Tudgeman's close personal friends, brushed past them in a floor-length brown Dwarflord cape.

"Princess Candlewick," Gordo said quickly to Veruca, "I figured out the Circlestone Code." Gordo handed the sheet of paper he had been staring at over to Veruca.

Veruca's face lit up. "Omigosh!" she cried. "Now we can get into the Dragonchamber! And then we can battle the man with the iron fist, after we go through the Eighth Vortex twice." Veruca was still babbling about the game as she and Gordo walked off down the hallway.

Lizzie and Miranda exchanged a look.

This was not good.

"Hey, Gordo," Lizzie said as she slid into the seat across from his at their usual table on the lunch patio. Gordo's face was hidden behind an enormous copy of the *Dwarflord Companion Guide*.

Gordo grunted at Lizzie without looking up.

Miranda frowned at Lizzie. "We thought we'd have lunch with you," Miranda said, leaning forward.

"Unnh," Gordo grunted.

Lizzie narrowed her eyes at him. For some reason, she got the impression that he wasn't even paying attention to what she and Miranda were saying. "There's ground-up eyeballs in the chili today," Lizzie said brightly.

"Unnh," Gordo replied.

Okay, that's it, Lizzie thought. "Gordo!" she snapped, yanking the Dwarflord book away from his face. But when she saw him, Lizzie gasped. His skin was pale and he had dark circles under his eyes.

Yikes! Okay, i see what the problem is—Gordo died a few weeks ago, and he didn't bother to tell us.

"Gordo, what's with the dark circles?" Miranda demanded. "You look like a raccoon."

Yeah, like a raccoon who's been playing way too much Dwarflord, Lizzie added mentally. "Are you getting *any* sleep at *all*?"

"No time," Gordo said with a wild look in his eyes. He held his finger and thumb a centimeter apart. "I'm this close to solving the Riddle of the Silver Hammer," he said.

"And, where's your lunch?" Lizzie asked, looking around. No sign of Gordo's food anywhere—not a crumb.

Gordo squinted at her dangerously. "I told you—Silver Hammer. Quit being a Nagworm."

Lizzie frowned. "But—"

"Yeah, Lizzie—quit being such a Nagworm," Miranda cut her off, her voice a dead-on imitation of Gordo's. Miranda rolled her eyes. "Sheesh!"

Lizzie sat back in her chair. Clearly, this situation was a lot worse than she had thought.

Over the next few days, Lizzie watched Gordo like a hawk. What she saw was not a pretty sight. In English class, Gordo spent the entire hour sketching a picture of a castle, and drawing arrows pointing to the best points of entry. In Math, he swapped Dwarflord cards with Larry and a few other Dwarfies. And he spent all of Social Studies reading his *Dwarflord Companion Guide* behind his textbook.

For a couple of days, Lizzie and Miranda played it cool, telling each other that Gordo would lose interest. But Gordo never called them anymore. He never wanted to hang out and watch movies, or go to the mall. This *is* getting serious, Lizzie finally admitted to herself.

"Hey, McG," Gordo said as he walked up to Lizzie in the hallway on Wednesday. "Sorry I ragged on you the other day. I was out of line."

Lizzie's heart thudded. Was Gordo finally back? "It's okay," she said sincerely. "I was just worried about you. You have to eat."

"I know, I know," Gordo said eagerly. "That's why I was hoping maybe I could borrow a couple bucks and get a turkey burger."

Lizzie frowned. Gordo's parents gave him a decent allowance and he was usually careful about how he spent it—he always had way more cash than she or Miranda did. "You don't have any money?" Lizzie asked. "Did you spend all your cash on those stupid Dwarf game-card thingies?"

"Yeah, yeah, I wasn't thinking clearly," Gordo admitted, looking at the ground sheepishly. Then he looked up at Lizzie with a hopeful expression. "That's why a turkey burger would be good—get some food in me."

"Okay," Lizzie said. Her eyebrows drew together in concern as she dug in her purse. "Here." She pulled a ten-dollar bill out of her pink wallet and handed it to Gordo. "And get some sleep, too, okay? You're falling apart."

"Yeah, yeah, I will," Gordo said quickly. "Thanks. See you." He turned and scurried down the hall.

Suspicion edged up Lizzie's spine as she watched him hurry off. Something about that interaction was seriously weird, Lizzie thought.

As he rounded the corner, Gordo glanced over his shoulder to make sure that Lizzie hadn't followed him. Then he walked up to a tall kid wearing a T-shirt that read: MY PARENTS VISITED THE REALM OF THE DWARFLORD, AND ALL I GOT WAS THIS LOUSY T-SHIRT. The kid's name was Ralph Sklar, and word was that he had some serious Dwarflord goods.

"Hey!" Gordo said as he hurried up to Ralph. "You still got the Gold Edition Dragon Monarch card?"

Ralph flashed Gordo a brilliant smile. "You got the money?"

Gordo handed over Lizzie's ten dollars plus ten more of his own. Ralph handed him the card, and they both touched their fists to their hearts, and then to their foreheads. "Huzzah!" said the Dwarfies.

Gordo kissed the Gold Edition Dragon Monarch card and walked away.

With his eyes trained on the card, he didn't even notice that Miranda was standing nearby—and she had seen the whole thing.

CHAPTER FIVE

"**N**ot bad," Lizzie said as she walked out of Social Studies holding the quiz that Mr. Escobar had just handed back. "B-plus."

"Me, too. The only one I got wrong was 'Where's the English Channel?'" Miranda gave Lizzie a mischievous grin. "I thought it was next to ESPN."

Lizzie giggled.

"How about you, Gordo?" Miranda asked.

"Oh, I got an A," Gordo said absently.

Not surprising, Lizzie thought. Gordo always got As.

Just then, the Dwarf Tribe appeared.

"Glimmerfoe!" Larry called. "Join us—Princess Candlewick has acquired the alabaster Dragon Egg." Veruca held up an oversized plastic egg.

Who knows what kind of freaky Dwarflord animal could be growing in there? Lizzie thought.

But Gordo looked really excited, as though the alabaster Dragon Egg were made of pure gold. "Oh, cool!" He dropped his test and headed off with the Tribe.

Lizzie watched Gordo walk away as Miranda leaned over and picked up the test.

"We've lost Gordo," Lizzie said sadly. "He's obsessed with Dwarflord."

Miranda shook her head. "It's worse than that." She handed Lizzie the test. There was more red on the paper than Santa Claus wears on Christmas!

"Gordo got an *F*?" Lizzie cried. But that's impossible! she thought. Gordo is a straight-A student! With wide eyes, Lizzie stared after the retreating Dwarf Tribe. They had completely surrounded Gordo.

Almost as though he could sense her look, Larry looked back over his shoulder and frowned at Lizzie. Then he waved his hands in another Dwarf Spell.

That spell may not be working on me, Lizzie thought, but it's definitely working on Gordo.

"Okay, I'm here," Gordo said to Lizzie and Miranda as he walked into Lizzie's house later that day. "Let's play." He looked around. "Where are your game pieces?"

"We don't have any," Lizzie said impatiently.

Lizzie's little brother Matt was lying on the couch, listening to the whole conversation. It did not sound good.

"But your message said you wanted to play Dwarflord." Gordo was clearly confused. "You said you wanted me to teach you."

Lizzie folded her arms across her chest. "Yeah, well, there's a simple explanation for that," she said.

"We lied," Miranda chimed in.

"Just as you've been lying about your grades," Lizzie agreed, "and what you're doing with your lunch money. Oh, I'm sorry, I mean, *my* lunch money."

"Fine," Gordo snapped. "You don't want me to borrow your lunch money anymore, I won't."

Lizzie gaped at her friend. Since when had supersmart Gordo become so super-dense? she wondered. "That's not it, Gordo. We just don't want you to play Dwarflord anymore. Okay? It's taken over your life."

Gordo scoffed, "It has not."

"Has so," Miranda countered.

Gordo raised a fist in the air. "I swear on the Sacred Shield of Olwen Thundereater it has not!" He paused for a moment. "All right, maybe that didn't sound so good. But, I know what I'm doing."

"We don't think you do," Lizzie told him. "We want you to go back to normal. We want you to stop."

"No." Gordo shrugged.

Is he serious? Lizzie wondered. Would he really choose a stupid board game over me and Miranda?

"Look, I can stop playing any time I want to," Gordo insisted. "But I'm not going to do it just because you say so." He held up his hands. "I'm outta here."

With that, Gordo turned and strode out of the house.

Matt stood up. "Man, that's one bad Dwarflord jones," he noted.

Lizzie gave him a skeptical look. "What do you know about it?"

Matt shrugged. "It's a cool game, but it can take you down a bad road. Last year, Lanny was seriously on the Dwarf. Spent all his money on collector's cards, talked nonstop about his characters . . ." That's definitely saying something, Lizzie thought, being that Lanny never says a word!

Matt nodded knowingly. "That Dwarflord is bad medicine."

Lizzie sighed. "I just hope he'll get over it."

"You can hope," Matt said. "And you can hope a grizzly bear doesn't eat you if you rub yourself with bacon. Gordo's a Dwarfhead— he needs help."

"So will you help him?" Miranda asked hopefully.

Lizzie's breath caught in her throat. Has it really come to this? she wondered. Are we seriously asking my brother for help? Gordo must *really* be in trouble.

Matt nodded. "It won't be easy," he warned. "It'll be intense. It'll be ugly. But Gordo helped me that time I got my head stuck in the banister. I owe him."

CHAPTER SIX

"I hate to bother you," Mrs. Sanchez said as she followed Mrs. McGuire into the backyard. "But I really think Edward left his cell phone at home on purpose so I couldn't call him." Mr. McGuire and Mr. Sanchez had spent every weekday evening and all day on the weekends sitting on the branch, watching the eggs.

Mrs. McGuire laughed. "Edward," she called into the tree, "your wife is here."

"Oooh!" Mr. Sanchez groaned.

"Standing right next to me," Mrs. McGuire clarified.

"Oooh!" Mr. Sanchez said again, pretending to be delighted this time.

"Edward, you've been over here for four hours now," Mrs. Sanchez scolded. "Remember you promised to clean the rain gutters?"

Mr. Sanchez scowled at his wife. "I want to watch the eggs!" he insisted.

"I really think it's time for you to come home now," Mrs. Sanchez replied.

"No!"

"Eduardo," Mrs. Sanchez said in a warning tone, *"vamanos."*

"No quiero!"

"Sam, maybe you ought to come down, too," Mrs. McGuire suggested gingerly.

"I don't wanna!" Mr. McGuire insisted. He eyed the bag of potato chips in her hand. "Just give us our potato chips."

"All right." Mrs. McGuire sighed. "I'll come up there."

"No! No girls allowed!" Mr. Sanchez insisted.

Mr. McGuire chimed in, "Yeah!" They had their own exclusive boys' club up in that tree.

"So . . ." Mrs. McGuire turned to Mrs. Sanchez and gave her a bright smile. "You want to go to the day spa?"

"Sure," Mrs. Sanchez said, grinning. "I've got Edward's credit card."

The girls' club joined hands and hurried out of the backyard.

Lizzie, Miranda, and Matt hurried over to Hillridge Junior High. They figured the Dwarf Tribe was probably still playing their game. And Gordo would, no doubt, be with them. Lizzie had told her parents that she would be back before dinner—and that Matt was helping them with a "special project." Project Deprogram Gordo, Lizzie thought as she peered around a corner.

A Dwarf Triber was standing at the door to the Social Studies room, which the Tribe used for their after-school meetings. The guard was wearing a hooded brown cloak and holding a staff and a spear.

"Just as I thought," Matt said knowingly. "They've posted sentries outside the game chamber. These are hard-core Dwarfies. Miranda—you know what to do."

Miranda nodded firmly and sashayed down the hallway. She stopped in front of the sentry and gave him a flirty smile. "Hi."

The Dwarfie gulped. "Hi."

"That's a really great outfit," Miranda lied, eyeing the fake-fur cloak.

Lizzie rolled her eyes. This kid's hideous brown cloak hadn't been in fashion since 1248, if it was even cool back then.

But the Dwarfie had no clue. "Really?" he asked.

Miranda nodded. "Yeah. I've always had a thing for . . ." She looked the kid up and down. "What are you, again?"

"Half elf, half badger," the Dwarfie prompted.

"For one of those," Miranda said.

Lizzie's heart went out to her friend as she watched Miranda chat with the sentry. Ugh, Lizzie thought, Miranda must really care about Gordo a lot if she's willing to flirt with a half elf. Lizzie was glad that her job was a lot less creepy.

But Miranda was really playing it up. She put her hand against her heart. "Pitter-patter," she said. "Oh, listen, could you show me where the nearest water fountain is?" She pressed her palm against her cheek, then fanned herself. "I'm feeling kind of warm. . . ."

The Dwarfie nodded eagerly. "A quest I would fain undertake, fair damsel."

Miranda smiled blankly. "Yuh-huh . . ."

"I won my spurs in the Gremlin Wars of the Twelfth Dimension," the sentry told Miranda as he led her down the hall, "when I—"

Just then, Lizzie and Matt jumped out of the janitor's closet, grabbed the elf-badger, and dragged him inside with them.

A moment later, Matt walked out of the closet followed closely by Lizzie, who was wearing the sentry's brown cloak. His itchy, *stinky* brown cloak, Lizzie said to herself as she adjusted the hood that—thankfully—hid her face. For one thing, she didn't want any of the other Dwarfies to suspect that she and Miranda were about to bust Gordo out of their mind-melting game. For another, Lizzie thought as she looked at the cloak, I don't want anyone to see me in this thing!

"You're half elf, half badger," Miranda whispered as she, Lizzie, and Matt tiptoed toward the sentry's post. "You won your spurs in the Gremlin wars."

Lizzie sniffed the cloak. "I wish I had time for a bath," she said sourly. "I smell like a petting zoo."

They reached the Social Studies classroom, and Matt slowly cracked the door open and peered inside. Everyone was wearing their Dwarflord getups. Larry was even wearing a crazy helmet with horns on it. It's like a bizarre-o fashion show, Lizzie thought. And, of course, Gordo was there, too.

"A great thirst grows upon me—" Larry announced. "The Wizard of the Woodglen craves a break. Princess Candlewick—prepare the Dwarf Brew."

Veruca nodded and stirred some disgusting-looking brown liquid in a crystal bowl.

"How are we supposed to get Gordo out of there?" Lizzie whispered.

"That Dwarf Brew they're drinking," Matt explained, as he pulled the door shut, "it's strong iced tea. Gordo Glimmerfoe's going to need a pit stop any time now. Okay, here's what we do—"

Lizzie leaned in to hear the plan. This was getting good.

Lizzie was standing with her back to the door as Gordo walked out of the Game Chamber.

"It's off to the watering trench, my half-badger brethren," Gordo said heartily, slapping Lizzie on the back.

The moment he turned toward the boys' room, Matt and Miranda ran up behind him and tossed a blanket around him. Gordo cried out, but they held him tightly.

"You're tickling me," Gordo complained, his voice muffled through the folds of the blanket.

Matt rolled up a trash can, and he, Miranda, and Lizzie hoisted Gordo into it. Then they turned the can on its side and began rolling it down the hallway.

"Don't jostle me—" Gordo cried. "I have to go to the bathroom!"

Lizzie winced. So, okay, this was slightly cruel and definitely unusual . . . but they were doing it for Gordo's own good.

"Careful—" Miranda said as they rolled the can around a corner, "we're losing it!"

Thud! Thud! Thud!

The garbage can bounced down the stairs, and Lizzie, her brother, and Miranda sprinted after it.

Poor Gordo yelped as he bounced down each step.

"This is not helping the bathroom situation at all!" Gordo wailed from inside the trash can.

CHAPTER SEVEN

Lizzie looked down at Gordo, who sat tied to an armchair facing a television screen in the center of the dim AV room. Matt had stuck bandages with wires attached to them to Gordo's arms. The wires didn't actually lead to anywhere, and Lizzie had no idea what they were supposed to do, but she decided to let her brother roll with it.

Lizzie wondered whether any of Gordo's Dwarfie buddies would notice he was gone. She could just imagine Larry Tudgeman walking out of the Social Studies room, calling out "Glimmerfoe? Art thou still in the bathroom?" I guess it doesn't matter, Lizzie figured. They'll never look for him *here*.

"What are you doing to me?" Gordo demanded.

"We're *helping* you," Lizzie told him.

"How is *this* helping me?" Gordo snapped.

"Dwarflord!" Matt shouted as he ripped off one of Gordo's sticky bandages.

Gordo winced and glared at Matt. "Ow!"

"Dwarflord!" Matt screeched, ripping off another bandage. "Dwarflord!" *Rip!* "This is aversion therapy," Matt explained to Gordo. "The thing you like causes you pain. Therefore you don't like it any more."

Gordo glanced down at the bandages. "What are the wires for?"

"The wires are for absolutely nothing," Matt said. "They just look pretty cool."

Lizzie stared at her brother. Did I ever actually think that Cactus Head knew what he was doing? she wondered.

"Look, if you don't cut this out, I'm gonna cause *you* pain," Gordo said threateningly, as he scowled at Matt.

"Okay, moving on to the next step," Matt said, clearly persuaded by Gordo's reasoning.

Miranda leaned over and ripped off one of Gordo's bandages.

"Ow!" Gordo glared at her.

"I just wanted to do one." Miranda shrugged and flashed Lizzie a guilty look. "It looked fun."

"Why are you doing this?" Gordo challenged.

"Because we want you back the way you were." Lizzie's voice was pleading.

"Back in the old days," Miranda agreed, "when you ate, and slept, and talked like a normal person."

"Maybe I just like Dwarflord," Gordo said defensively.

"Well, maybe you do," Lizzie replied. "But if you don't change, you're gonna end up like this—" Matt thrust a big, glossy photo of a long-haired, lonely-looking guy into Gordo's face. "Alvin Steck," Lizzie explained. "He's a regional Dwarflord champion. He's thirty-six years old and he lives in his mother's basement."

Gordo grimaced.

"He works part-time at a barber shop, sweeping up hair," Miranda chimed in. "He hasn't had a date since his junior prom."

"He took *his cousin*," Lizzie added.

Gordo shuddered.

That's right, Lizzie thought. It's harsh stuff, but it's true.

"His whole life is Dwarflord," Miranda went on. "He's missed out on swimsuit calendars, curly fries, and souped-up motorcycles. . . ."

Matt pressed a button on the remote, and the television screen flickered on.

"Don't miss out, Gordo," Matt pleaded.

Beethoven's "Ode to Joy" rang from the speakers as Gordo watched images of himself play onscreen. He was doing things that he used to love—eating curly fries, listening to Rat Pack music, riding a unicycle, dancing with Lizzie and Miranda, playing football with Matt, having a waterfight, shooting movies . . .

Miranda thrust a bunch of photographs into Gordo's face: Lizzie, Miranda, and Gordo hanging out. Watching motocross racing. Goofing in the hallway.

Gordo blinked and looked back up at the video screen. The images kept coming: Fries. Hacky Sack. Dressing as Elvis. Hanging out. More fries. Pizza. Bowling. The Mall. Movies. More fries. Cool vintage clothes. And always those cursedly tempting fries, fries, fries!

"All right!" Gordo shouted. "Enough! Enough! French fries! French fries! Give me fries!"

Lizzie was ready for this. She held out a plate of fries and shoved one into Gordo's mouth. "Oh, how about we go to the lake tomorrow?" he asked as he munched away. "Anyone wanna watch basketball tomorrow night? Mmm, is there ketchup?"

"No," Lizzie told him.

Gordo didn't seem to care. Lizzie just kept shoveling fries into his mouth and Gordo kept munching as though he hadn't eaten in a week. Which, come to think of it, Lizzie realized, he may not have.

"The crisis has passed," Matt announced. "My work here is done." He bowed toward Gordo.

Lizzie smiled at her brother. For once, she thought, Matt had done something right!

CHAPTER EIGHT

"**Y**ou know what's really good?" Gordo said on Saturday morning. He and Miranda had come over to the McGuires' house for breakfast, and Gordo was currently shoveling sugary cereal into his mouth as quickly as possible. "You mix the Sugar-O's and Marshmallow Puffies—it's a very good combination."

Lizzie grinned. Yeah—that's a great combination, she thought. If you like sugar-coated sugar.

Gordo shoved his spoon back into the cereal mix—he didn't show any signs of slowing down on the munchathon he'd been engaging in for the past day and a half. "I say we do the mall today, and we can save the lake for next week, when it's supposed to be warmer."

Gordo's back! i mean, he still obsesses about stuff, but at least it's good stuff, like sports and junk food and helping me with my homework.

Lizzie giggled as she took a spoonful of cereal. "Sounds good to me, Gordo."

"And when we're at the beach, we can get curly fries!" Gordo said happily.

Miranda studied Gordo for a moment. "Dwarflord!" she shouted.

"Ow!" Gordo cried, wincing and rubbing his arm.

Miranda turned back to her cereal. "Just checking."

"Everybody!" Mr. McGuire called from the backyard. "Come quick!"

"Yes, hurry!" Mr. Sanchez agreed.

Lizzie shoved back her chair. It was only ten o'clock in the morning, but already her dad and Miranda's dad were up in that tree.

"Come on, the eggs are hatching!" Mr. McGuire shouted as the three friends walked into the backyard, followed by Mrs. McGuire, who was still in her bathrobe.

"Hurry!" Mr. Sanchez gaped at the eggs eagerly. "Their little beaks are breaking through!" He grinned at Mr. McGuire. "We're fathers!"

Lizzie raised an eyebrow.

"Kids, you should really see this!" Lizzie's dad called. "Nature is such a miracle!"

Lizzie stared at him. *The real miracle is how Dad managed to sit on that branch for so long without it breaking,* Lizzie thought.

"Look," Mr. McGuire cried, still staring at the eggs, "one's poking its head out. . . . It's black!"

"They're crows!" Mr. Sanchez said. "Cute . . . little . . . crows."

There was a squawk, and Mr. McGuire looked up. "Hey," he said, "that must be the mother. Looks like she's in a hurry."

Mr. Sanchez nodded. "She looks . . . angry."

Suddenly, Mr. Sanchez's eyes grew wide and he let out a cry as the mother bird flew directly at his head. There was more loud squawking and lots of pecking as the two dads tried to fight off the bird. Feathers flew everywhere!

Then: *Thud. Thud.*

Mr. Sanchez and Mr. McGuire dropped right out of the tree and landed on the soft grass of the McGuires' back lawn.

Mrs. McGuire winced. "Oh—I'll get some ice packs," she said, hurrying toward the rear door.

Just then, Matt wandered out into the backyard. "Is my school project done yet?" he wanted to know.

Mr. McGuire rolled over onto his back. He was covered in black feathers. "It's done," he said, grunting. "I think I sprained my shoulder."

Matt's eyes grew wide. "Cool. My next project is first aid!" Matt knelt next to Mr. McGuire and poked him in the arm.

"Ow!"

Matt poked again.

"Ow!"

"Dad, that's fun," Matt said.

Mr. McGuire smiled at him wearily.

Well, Lizzie thought as she watched them, at least Matt has found a school project that interests him.

"Uh . . . you guys ready to go to the mall?" Lizzie asked her friends.

Miranda nodded. "Sounds good."

Gordo took a deep breath. "Ah, the mall. No trolls, no wizards. Just cinnamon buns, the arcades." He smiled at Lizzie and Miranda. "And you guys. Thanks for pulling me back."

Lizzie shrugged. "Sure." Then she waved her hands and waggled her fingers, and said in her best Dwarflord-spell-voice, "But, now you get to pay for the cinnamon buns!"

Gordo laughed. Really laughed.

He's back! Lizzie realized. Back for good. And there wasn't a half elf/half badger in the world that could change him!

PART
TWO

CHAPTER ONE

Lizzie frowned at the vat of green glop that bubbled away sinisterly behind the cafeteria counter. I think it's supposed to be goulash, Lizzie thought, but it looks like plain old "goo."

"What is this stuff?" she asked her best friend, Miranda. Lizzie took a sniff.

Ooh, Lizzie realized as the stench reached her nose, that was a mistake.

"Uh, looks like another potato-chips-and-cake day," Miranda said as she eyed the soup.

"I see you guys decided to pass on the daily special," Gordo said as he walked up to Lizzie and Miranda. He had a video camera in his hand and was filming them. Gordo was always filming people around the school—he claimed that he never knew when he was going to get good material, so he always wanted to be ready.

Lizzie looked skeptical as Gordo captured her image on film. "You mean the goulash surprise?" she asked. Like Gordo really thought they would go for *that*.

"I don't like surprises," Miranda said, curling her lip and waving away the foul-food smell. "Especially not goulash ones."

Lizzie nodded as she followed Miranda out of the serving area. Birthday surprises—yes. Fabulous shopping surprises—yes. Goulash, meat loaf, or casserole anything surprises—pass.

Gordo swung his video camera so that it took in the entire cafeteria scene. "And now, the ritualistic dance known as Table Selection," he said in a hushed voice, as though he were a narrator for the Nature Channel.

Lizzie followed the gaze of Gordo's camera lens. The jocks were all sitting at one table. The Mathletes preferred the corner. And the skaters were near the window.

"Don't try to sit with the popular kids—they might rip your head off," Gordo said for his camera's benefit as he pulled his lens in tight on a table of popular kids. They ignored him.

Lizzie rolled her eyes. Doesn't Gordo know that it doesn't pay to have the popular table notice you? It's much better to slip by them, under their Verbal Abuse Radar.

"Jocks," Gordo said dryly as he focused on the athletes' table, where a kid sat with his leg in a cast. "Sure, if you like broken bones."

Finally, Gordo's camera tracked over to where the nerds were discussing parabolas. "Sit at the loser table and you risk the rejection of the rest of the herd."

Lizzie could just imagine the sound effects Gordo would drop in later—roaring lions for the jocks, cash registers ringing for the cheerleaders. He enjoyed doing stuff like that. He said that it added another dimension to the film.

Whatever, Lizzie decided as she sat down at an empty table. Just as long as he doesn't add in any sounds for me and Miranda.

"Gordo," Miranda said, "lunch is horrifying enough without recording it."

Sighing, Gordo put down his camera. Then he plopped into the chair opposite Miranda. "Of course lunch is horrible," Gordo noted. "No one ever said middle school would be easy."

At that moment, snobby Kate Sanders walked by. She was wearing a pink skirt and a pink sweater and looked absolutely perfect, as usual. Lizzie rolled her eyes. Kate used to be Lizzie's best friend—until Kate discovered popularity. Now she was the Princess Snide and dissed Lizzie and her friends whenever she had the chance.

Ignoring Lizzie, Kate beamed at her cheerleader friends and waved. Then she took her usual seat at the popular table.

Lizzie bit her lip, thinking about Gordo's comment. Kate sure made middle school look like a piece of cake. Maybe she never got the "Middle School is Rough" memo, Lizzie thought. "Yeah, somebody tell that to Kate," Lizzie said miserably.

"Look, how many times do I have to tell you that one day Kate's life will be meaningless and miserable?" Gordo demanded.

Lizzie sighed. She knew that Gordo was right. But still . . .

. . . it's just so hard to wait.

The minute the bell rang, Lizzie, Gordo, and Miranda headed out of the lunchroom toward their lockers. But once they were out of the cafeteria Gordo suddenly stopped in his tracks. "Wait, where's my camera?" he asked once.

Miranda and Lizzie exchanged a look. It

wasn't like Gordo to wander off without his video camera. The thing was practically attached to the end of his arm.

"You must have left it in the cafeteria," Lizzie said.

"Okay, wait here," Gordo commanded. "I'll go back and see if it's there."

Gordo trotted back through the swinging doors.

"You think he'll find it?" Miranda asked.

"If he doesn't, we'll be having it for lunch tomorrow," Lizzie replied, shuddering at the thought. The scary thing was, with the food they served at Hillridge's cafeteria, it was totally possible.

"Remember the time I lost my bracelet?" Miranda said.

Lizzie grimaced. "Oh, and I had it in my mac and cheese the next day?"

"Gross!" Lizzie and Miranda said together.

Lizzie made a face and stuck out her tongue.

Just then, Gordo trotted up with the camera. "It was on the whole time," he said, peering at the video screen. "You guys will *never* believe what I got on tape," he said, clearly excited.

Miranda's eyes brightened. "Elvis?" she asked.

"Bigfoot?" Lizzie suggested.

"Close," Gordo said pointing to Lizzie. "Kate."

Lizzie smiled. This could be good. "Cool," she said, leaning in to catch a glimpse of the video screen. Sure enough, Kate was sitting there with Claire Miller, her best friend. Lizzie liked to think of Claire as the Vice-Snob. She didn't have as much power as Kate did, but was still an important figurehead.

"Okay, promise you won't tell anyone?" Kate whispered on-screen.

Claire leaned in a little closer. "Sure," she said. "What is it?"

"I'm a year older than everybody," Kate confessed.

"You are?" Claire asked.

Kate nodded. "Yeah."

Lizzie nearly gasped. How could that be true? Lizzie had known her practically forever, and Kate had always claimed that they were the same age. . . .

On the monitor, Claire was having the same reaction. Claire's eyes were wide. "But you're in our grade!"

"Remember," Kate whispered fiercely, "you promised not to tell anyone."

"You mean you got held back?" Claire asked.

Lizzie and her friends stared at one another, then cracked up.

"It was only in kindergarten!" Kate wailed.

Claire shrugged. "I guess that's not so bad, right?"

Kate looked around nervously, to be sure that no one was listening. "I've been hiding this ever since elementary school," she admitted. "If anybody finds out I'm a year older than everybody else, my whole image will be totally ruined." Looking worried, Kate pressed a manicured hand against her neck and pursed her lips.

Then the screen went fuzzy—the tape was over. Lizzie stood there for a moment, stunned. "I cannot believe that Kate was held back in kindergarten," she said, genuinely shocked.

What did she do? Fail nap time?

Miranda shook her head in admiration as the three friends started down the hall. "Prepare your speech, Gordo," she said. "This is your award winner."

"I can't believe it," Gordo said, staring at his video camera in amazement. "I finally get something good, and it's completely by accident." He looked down at his camera, his eyebrows drawn together as though he were thinking hard. "Wait, maybe I can get some more of this."

"What do you mean?" Lizzie asked.

"More of this hidden-camera stuff," Gordo said quickly, his eyes gleaming with excitement. "This has incredible potential."

Gordo's right, Lizzie realized. He could find out the dirt on everybody! Finally—one of Gordo's weird hobbies was coming in handy!

CHAPTER TWO

"**H**ey, Dad," Lizzie's brother Matt said as he walked into the living room. His parents were flopped on the couch, staring at the television set. Maybe that's why they didn't notice Matt's outfit. He was wearing a football helmet, and had used two of Mr. McGuire's best belts to strap pillows to himself—one on his chest and one on his back. "Would you run me over with the car?" Matt asked.

"Sure," Mr. McGuire said absently, his eyes

still glued to the TV screen, "in a minute, son."

Mrs. McGuire stared at her husband. "Sam!"

"What?" Mr. McGuire asked, totally clueless. He turned to his wife. "What did I do?"

"Mom, chill," Matt said, leaning over the arm of the couch. "It's for school."

"Oh," Mrs. McGuire said as she nodded. "I am *so* looking forward to hearing you explain this."

Matt sighed and shook his head. "Mom, Mom, Mom, Mom, Mom," he said in a patronizing voice. "Haven't you ever heard of Career Day?"

Mrs. McGuire eyed Matt's outfit without cracking a smile. "What kind of career is this?" she demanded. "Insurance fraud?"

"No," Matt replied, "stuntman."

"Cool," Mr. McGuire said.

Mrs. McGuire glared at her husband.

"No, not cool," Mr. McGuire corrected himself. "Very not cool."

Mrs. McGuire turned back to her son. "Why can't you be a doctor or a lawyer?"

"That would require years of schooling," Matt pointed out. "This I can do right now."

"Matt, we are not running you over with the car," Mrs. McGuire said in her "That's Final" voice.

"Fine," Matt said, clearly disappointed. "I'll come up with something else."

The next day at school, Gordo placed his video camera in a cabinet at the back of the science lab, leaving the door open just a little. He hated to leave his camera anywhere unsafe, but the opportunity to get the goods on practically everyone at school was just too tempting to resist. He walked out of the room as students started to stream in. Gordo tried to look casual, but he just couldn't help smiling a little.

That afternoon, Gordo climbed the tree outside the stairwell window and left his camera pointed right at the kids passing by. Then he waited until the bell rang and let the camera roll.

The next day, Gordo hid his video camera in a locker. And the day after that, in the school garbage can, stuffed beneath a pile of newspapers. Then it was between a couple of books on the library shelf. Then the school trophy case, and after that, a hollowed-out loaf of cafeteria bread.

Gordo knew he was going to get something good. And he could hardly wait to find out what it was!

"Okay," Gordo said as he punched a button on the VCR remote and settled down onto the McGuires' couch between Lizzie and Miranda, "let's see what we got."

He reached for a handful of popcorn as the television screen came on.

Oh. My. Lizzie thought as she watched one of Kate's queen-bee snob friends walk up the stairwell. She paused right in front of Gordo's camera and fixed a wedgie. A moment later, Lizzie watched as a popular boy picked his nose behind a library book.

This is even better than I imagined! Lizzie thought as she looked at Miranda and the two cracked up.

Next up, two huge jocks stood talking by their lockers. "Okay," the bigger kid asked his friend, "you really want to know my secret?"

The other guy nodded. "Yeah."

"I'll tell you." The big jock looked around to make sure that no one was looking. Then he yanked open his locker and pulled out a pink stuffed bunny. "Here," he said, holding out the stuffed animal to his buddy, "pet it." The other jock was skeptical. "Just pet the bunny," the bigger jock insisted. "I tell you, I do it every time before a game. It'll bring you luck."

Lizzie had to fight to keep from laughing. She didn't want to miss a second of this video!

The scene switched to the cafeteria. A pretty girl took a long sip from a can of soda and let out a very looooong burp. She quickly covered her mouth with her hand and looked around to see whether anybody had been watching.

The three friends on the couch laughed. Nobody was watching . . . nobody but us! Lizzie thought.

Lizzie couldn't stop giggling again at the burp. "Gordo," she said between laughs, "that was great."

"Do you realize what you have here?"

Miranda demanded as she gestured toward the TV screen. "Do you even know what would happen if other people in school saw this stuff?"

Gordo nodded. "Yeah. They'd know what I've always known. That even the popular kids have stuff to be embarrassed about."

"Gordo," Lizzie insisted, "you've got to figure out a way to get everyone to see this."

She thought about how Gordo was always promising her that Kate's life would one day be empty and meaningless. Why wait? Lizzie thought. She and her popular friends can be miserable right now—thanks to the miracle of modern technology!

Gordo nodded, and Lizzie smiled. This was going to be great.

CHAPTER THREE

Mr. McGuire walked out of the house right after Matt, who was holding an umbrella and a pillow. Matt had leaned a ladder against the house. He plumped up the pillow and set it a few feet from the bottom of the ladder. Then he headed up the ladder, still carrying the umbrella.

"Matt," Mr. McGuire said, as he peered up at his son.

"Yes?"

"Come down here right now," Mr. McGuire commanded.

"As soon as I open up the umbrella, Dad," Matt promised. His latest plan was to fly around the backyard like Mary Poppins—or, rather, like Mary Poppins's stunt double.

"No, son," Mr. McGuire said patiently, "you're going to use the ladder."

"Oh, man!" Matt griped. But he climbed down the ladder anyway.

Mr. McGuire gestured toward his son. "Come on, give me the umbrella." He shook his head as Matt handed over the umbrella. "I can't believe it. These things never work. Trust me, I know." This was true. Mr. McGuire had tried plenty of stunts when he was Matt's age—and they had all turned out badly.

"What about sheets for a parachute?" Matt suggested.

"Even worse," Mr. McGuire replied. "Gets wrapped around your face."

Matt watched his father walk back into the house. He knew there had to be a stunt he could do. He just needed to figure out what it was.

"Look! Look!" Gordo shouted as he ran up to Lizzie and Miranda in the school hallway. He thrust a flyer at them gasping, "This is it! I know exactly where my film's going to show!"

Lizzie peered at the flyer. "'Unified School District 41 Student Film Competition,'" she read aloud. The page was covered with instructions for entering the contest.

Miranda's dark eyebrows disappeared beneath the perfectly straight line of her bangs. "Where did you get this?"

"Off the bulletin board." Gordo grinned.

"You read the bulletin board?" Miranda gave him a dubious look.

Lizzie looked blank. "We *have* a bulletin board?"

"I think that I have the ultimate real-life documentary about middle school," Gordo gushed, ignoring the sarcastic bulletin board comments.

"You're a lock, Gordo," Miranda said confidently. "Your film is gonna be great."

Lizzie nodded. There was only one thing she was dying to know. "So," she said brightly, "where is this so-called bulletin board?"

Lizzie was sitting by herself with her lunch tray when Miranda came storming onto the patio. She rammed into a guy, knocking his tray over. "Move it!" Miranda growled.

Lizzie frowned at her friend as Miranda threw herself into the chair across from her. "Where's your lunch?"

"To have lunch you need money," Miranda

snarled. "Which I left in my backpack. Which I left on the bus this morning. Along with my third-period book report and my clean gym clothes. Someone put gum on my locker, and to top it all off, I just found out Larry Tudgeman uses my picture as a screen saver on his computer." Miranda slumped in her seat.

Lizzie curled her lip at the thought of being Tudgeman's screen saver. That alone would make Miranda's day qualify for the top five on the worst-mornings-of-all-time list. "Well," she said brightly, "Want some of my french fries?" Lizzie held the fries out to her friend, but Miranda just glared at them.

"Why don't they just slap a big sign on this school that says 'Loser Farm' and be done with it?" Miranda demanded, gesturing wildly.

"You're having a really bad day," Lizzie said soothingly. "But school isn't *that* bad."

"You're right," Miranda said, her voice

dripping with sarcasm, "it's not 'that bad.' It's *terrible*. Everyone looks up to the jocks and the cheerleaders, who are a bunch of stuck-up dirks who are going to end up working the drive-through at Burger Buddy."

Lizzie pushed away her tray. "Okay. Vent."

"It's this whole place," Miranda griped. "It's the way people say one thing to your face and another behind your back." Lizzie nodded sympathetically, but Miranda was just getting warmed up. She had plenty of words about her school—all of them harsh. It went on for a long time, longer than Lizzie would have thought possible.

Back at home, Matt stood on the landing tying a pair of his mother's stockings to his ankle. The other end was already tied to the banister. It was the setup for his latest stunt idea: stocking-bungee jumping.

"Matt?" Mr. McGuire said as he walked by. "Don't use your mother's stockings for bungee jumping."

Matt sighed and untied the stockings. He'd been expecting his father to nix his idea, but that was okay. He had a better one, anyway.

Matt grabbed a hula hoop from Lizzie's room and hurried down to the kitchen, where he started searching through the pantry. "Hey, Dad, do we have a blowtorch?" Matt asked his father.

"Son, you're not jumping through a ring of fire," Mr. McGuire replied.

Matt groaned. He just couldn't figure out why his dad didn't like any of his ideas. Matt knew that if he wanted parental permission for his Career Day project, he would have to come up with something really good.

A little while later, Matt Rollerbladed through the hallway. He was wearing a helmet, and had strapped a leaf blower to his back. The helmet was really the key to the whole stunt. Matt believed that nothing was really dangerous, as long as you had on a helmet. Not even leaf-blower jet packs!

Just then, Matt's parents walked into the hallway.

"Son," Mr. McGuire said, "don't use my leaf blower as a jet pack."

"How do you expect me to be a stuntman?" Matt wailed. "You won't let me do anything!"

"Find something else to be, Matt," Mrs. McGuire suggested patiently.

"Fine," Matt snapped. "Squash my dreams. I'll come up with something else."

CHAPTER FOUR

Lizzie settled on the couch next to Miranda and Gordo. It was time to view Gordo's latest collection of hidden-camera footage.

"I'm hoping for another big Kate revelation," Lizzie said cheerfully as she grabbed a handful of popcorn.

"I dunno," Miranda said doubtfully. "I'm a big fan of the pet-the-bunny boy."

The friends giggled as Gordo pointed the remote at the screen and pressed PLAY. "And today's digital dynamite is . . ."

"Why don't they just slap a big sign on this school that says 'Loser Farm' and be done with it?" a familiar voice demanded on screen.

Miranda sat up straight on the couch.

"That's Miranda, Gordo!" Lizzie cried, elbowing the filmmaker in the ribs.

Gordo nodded. "Yeah, it is."

Miranda looked shocked . . . and not too happy. "You taped me?"

Lizzie gulped.

i'd love to stick around, but i got, uhhh . . . a *thing!*

"It's terrible . . ." Miranda said on-screen.

"All I did was tape the Quad," Gordo said defensively. "I didn't know you were going to be there."

"It's okay," Lizzie said calmly. "It's no big deal." She gave Miranda a bright smile. "Your hair looked fab."

Miranda glared at her. "You're taking his side?" she demanded. Then she turned back to Gordo. "Who died and made you Big Brother, anyway?"

"You were happy to watch it when it was other people," Gordo pointed out.

"It's no big deal," Lizzie told Miranda, "it's not like he's gonna use this stuff."

Gordo gave Lizzie a frown. "Of course I am, why wouldn't I?"

"Because if anyone from school sees me on that tape, I'm toast!" Miranda barked.

Lizzie winced. She had a bad feeling that *Gordo* was about to be toast.

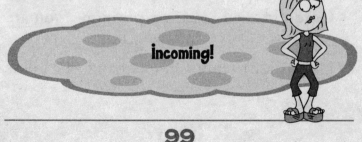

Incoming!

"I think you worry a little too much about what other people think," Gordo told Miranda as he tossed a popcorn kernel into his mouth.

Miranda narrowed her eyes. "Not everyone is like you. Some of us care what other people think." Then she stood up, threw a couch pillow down, and stormed out of the room.

"If you ask me, she's being a little hypocritical," Gordo said as Miranda slammed the front door on her way out.

"Come on, Gordo—" Lizzie said reasonably, "you know if anyone at school sees that tape, she can never show her face in school again."

"That's ridiculous," Gordo said dismissively. "People are going to love this."

Lizzie looked at him doubtfully.

Gordo studied Lizzie's expression. "You are on my side, aren't you?" he asked.

Lizzie didn't reply. On one hand, she knew

that Gordo had a point—Miranda shouldn't care what anyone thought of her. On the other hand, Lizzie thought, Miranda and I live in the real world, where having people hate you is seriously not fun.

Why do we have drills for fires and earthquakes, but nothing for when your two best friends declare war on each other?

* * *

Lizzie looked nervously around the Digital Bean, her favorite cybercafe. Miranda was at their usual table. Taking a deep breath, Lizzie hurried over to join her friend. "Oh, good. You're here," Lizzie said as she slid into the chair across from Miranda's. Lizzie forced herself to smile. She had some news for Miranda—some bad news—and Lizzie didn't want the conversation to get off on the wrong foot. She wanted Miranda to be able to put things into perspective. "You're always so punctual," Lizzie gushed. "And your hair looks incredible. Are those new earrings?"

"No," Miranda said slowly. "You gave them to me last year for my birthday. What's wrong with you?"

Lizzie let out her breath in a big whoosh. "You'd better sit down."

"Lizzie," Miranda said seriously, "look at me. I am sitting down."

"Right." Lizzie cleared her throat. "Um, well, I thought I should be the first one to tell you that Gordo's one of the finalists in the film competition."

Miranda let out a groan and grabbed the

edge of the table. "Oh, no. Have you seen the film? How bad was I? Do I need to transfer schools?"

"I haven't seen it yet," Lizzie admitted.

"I didn't even mean that stuff," Miranda wailed. "I was just having a bad day. Now all the school district officials are going to see me ragging on our school."

Lizzie swallowed hard, wondering whether something like this could go on a permanent record. "Actually," Lizzie corrected gently, "the whole school *district* is going to see you. They're showing all three final films at a big assembly."

"I'm dead," Miranda said miserably. "I'm the late Miranda Sanchez."

"What are you doing, sweetheart?" Mrs. McGuire asked, as she and her husband walked into the kitchen, where Matt was smashing hard candies with a meat tenderizer and putting them onto a cookie sheet.

Matt shrugged. "Cooking," he singsonged.

"See?" Mr. McGuire said to his wife. "This is good. No more stuntman stuff. He's going to be a chef."

Matt bashed another piece of candy.

"Hey, he can have his own restaurant. . . ." Mrs. McGuire said brightly.

"He could have his own cooking show. . . ." Mr. McGuire suggested, getting carried away with the thought. "*BAM!*" he said in his best Emeril voice.

Bam! Matt crushed another hard candy.

"Hey, we can go to his house for Thanksgiving!" Mrs. McGuire realized.

"Our son," Mr. McGuire said proudly, "the chef."

Mrs. McGuire watched her son as he continued to smash away at the candy.

"Don't tell him we like it," Mrs. McGuire whispered, "or he'll stop doing it."

Matt whacked the heck out of another piece of candy. It didn't look like he was going to stop "cooking" any time soon.

CHAPTER FIVE

"**S**o, the screening's sixth period," Gordo explained as he unpacked his backpack and placed his books in his locker, "but all the finalists have to be there by lunch."

"Okay, so you still have some time left," Lizzie said quickly. "Is there any way that you can cut out Miranda's part? You have so much other great footage." Lizzie's voice was pleading. She really, really wanted her best friends to be best friends again. All of this tension over a stupid movie was a serious bummer.

"Yeah, but the stuff with Miranda sort of ties it all together," Gordo pointed out as he shut his locker.

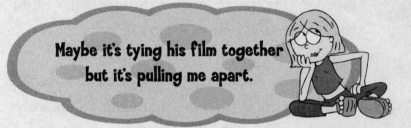

Maybe it's tying his film together but it's pulling me apart.

Just then, Ethan Craft walked up to Gordo and patted him on the back. "Hey, dude, I heard about your film," Ethan said warmly as he threw his arm around Gordo's shoulders. "Where's it playing?"

"In the A.V. room," Gordo said. "Sixth period."

"Oh, so it's not a real movie?" Ethan seemed disappointed.

"Yeah, Ethan," Gordo said with a straight

face. "I just made a thirty-five-million-dollar action movie and they're screening it at the assembly."

Ethan's face lit up. "Hey, way to go, Gordo!" He gave Gordo a thumbs-up. "I'll be there," he said before strutting away.

Lizzie sighed as Gordo shook his head. *Even when Ethan says something dumb,* she thought, *he somehow manages to make it seem adorable. . . . But I can't get distracted,* Lizzie reminded herself. *I have a friendship to save.* "Gordo, I meant I really don't think you should do this," Lizzie said in an attempt to get back on topic.

"Hey, Gordo," Kate said as she and her Vice-Snob Claire strutted up to Gordo, ignoring Lizzie. "Are we going to be in your movie?"

"How could he do a movie about our school without us?" Claire demanded, tossing her long dark hair over her shoulder.

Lizzie had to work hard to keep herself from laughing. "You don't know how true that is," she said.

"Well, good luck," Kate said, giving Gordo a little wave. "I'm sure it's gonna be great." She and Claire pranced away.

"Thanks!" Gordo said brightly, grinning at Kate and Claire. "I'll see you guys at the screening!"

Lizzie stared at her friend. "Gordo!" she pleaded, hoping he'd reconsider.

"Look, Lizzie, I gotta go," Gordo said. "But do me a favor—watch the movie before you tell me what I should or should not do."

Lizzie sighed as Gordo walked away. This is not going according to plan, she thought.

"Great," Miranda said miserably as she joined Lizzie in the hall. "Everyone in school's talking about this film and how they're going to see it. Gordo caught me on one bad day and now the whole school's going to think I'm a total loser."

"Maybe not," Lizzie said hopefully. "Maybe it's not as bad as we think. Gordo says that we should see it before we make up our minds."

Miranda's eyes narrowed to dangerous slits. "I can't believe it—you're taking Gordo's side?"

Lizzie shook her head. "I'm not taking anybody's side."

"Well, you should be," Miranda insisted. She pointed at herself. "You should be taking my side!"

That's what everybody wants! Lizzie thought.

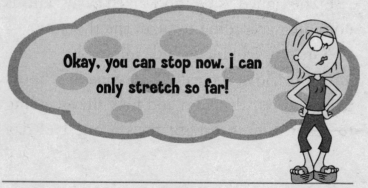

Okay, you can stop now. I can only stretch so far!

"Come on, Miranda," Lizzie begged, "you know that this is a big deal for Gordo."

"And it's a big moment for me," Miranda snapped. She stared at Lizzie with huge eyes. "It's the moment where my fate is sealed as a social outcast."

Lizzie's heart sank. Why did this good thing happening to Gordo have to turn into a bad thing for Miranda? Is that the way the world works? Lizzie wondered. You can't have the good without the bad? Because, if so, that seemed seriously unfair.

CHAPTER SIX

Matt fastened his helmet as he set up a large pane of colored glass in the backyard. It was the grand finale for his latest idea—a super-cool daredevil stunt course. Flat planks of wood circled the backyard in a U shape, and "Matt Rules" was scrawled across the track. Matt knew that this was going to be awesome. He was sure he'd get an A+ for Career Day.

"Matt," Mrs. McGuire said as she walked out onto the deck, "what are you doing?"

"What's it look like I'm doing?" Matt

replied. "I'm setting up my Mile of Death Ultimate Torture Track."

"Where did you get all the wood?" Mrs. McGuire asked as she stared at the stunt course. "What happened to cooking?"

"I was cooking the candy to make the fake glass to crash through," Matt explained, gesturing toward the multicolored candy glass pane that stood behind him.

Mrs. McGuire let out a disappointed sigh. "Uh, honey, I thought we agreed that you weren't going to be a stuntman."

"I'm not going to," Matt said. He grinned. "I'm going to be a *daredevil*."

Mrs. McGuire nodded. "Ah." She wasn't really sure how to reply. Sometimes her son's logic defied reasonable argument. Mrs. McGuire realized that she was going to need some help with this one. "SAM?" she shouted into the house.

"I'm a bit busy, hon," Mr. McGuire called back. "I'm ironing my pants."

"Well, I guess it's time for a test run," Matt said to his mom. He took a deep breath and walked toward the ramp that marked the beginning of his daredevil course. Matt got ready to launch himself on his skateboard. He knew that this was going to be awesome.

"Sam, you get out here AND I MEAN NOW!" Mrs. McGuire screeched.

Matt was making the final adjustments to his helmet strap as his dad scurried out of the house. Mr. McGuire was dressed for work— sort of. He was still pulling on his pants as he stumbled outside. Just as he stepped onto the deck, he tripped on one of his pant legs and belly flopped onto Matt's skateboard!

Mr. McGuire let out a yelp as the skateboard took off, hurling him onto the Torture Track. Mr. McGuire headed down the ramp, through two sheets of candy glass, through a pyramid of cereal boxes, and then he was launched toward a kiddie swimming pool . . . which he missed.

"Whoa!" Mr. McGuire shouted as he ran headfirst into the backyard fence.

Matt stared, wide-eyed, at his dad, who was now lying on his back in the yard. He had a lot of grass in his hair. "Yow," Matt said. "That's gotta hurt."

"Yeah," Mr. McGuire gasped.

"Okay, maybe I don't want to be a daredevil," Matt said slowly. He thought for a moment. What would he do now that he'd changed his mind about his entire future? What career could possibly compare to daredevil? After a moment, Matt had an idea. Something glamorous, but not nearly as dangerous. Matt played a little air guitar. "How about a rock star?"

Mr. McGuire sighed. Still, he had to admit to himself that he was glad that he'd shown Matt that he had been right all along—being a daredevil or a stuntman was dangerous work.

Dangerous and *painful.*

Back at the after-school assembly where Gordo's film was being shown, Lizzie tried to calm the butterflies in her stomach as she settled into the chair next to Gordo's. What would Miranda say afterward? Worse—what would the rest of the school say to Miranda? Lizzie had a bad feeling that things could get ugly. And the tension between Gordo and Miranda might be the least of it.

Lizzie looked at the empty seat beside her. On the other hand, she thought, where the heck *is* Miranda, anyway?

"I can't believe it," Gordo said with a

frown, "my debut as a director and here I am not wearing a baseball hat."

"Baseball bat, yeah," Lizzie said absently.

"Baseball *hat*," Gordo corrected, looking at Lizzie closely. "Are you okay?"

"Actually, no," Lizzie confessed as she picked up her backpack. "I'll be right back."

"You're gonna miss my movie," Gordo said, sounding worried.

"I won't," Lizzie assured him. "I promise." And I'm not going to let Miranda miss it, either, Lizzie thought as she hurried up the aisle.

Lizzie found Miranda outside in the hallway. "Hey," Lizzie said gently as she joined her friend.

"Hey," Miranda said. She glanced toward the A.V. room. "Why aren't you in there with 'Spielberg'?"

"Because I wanted to make sure that you're okay," Lizzie said.

"I'm fine, really," Miranda said sarcastically. "That's why I'm hiding from the entire school."

Mr. Escobar, Lizzie's Social Studies teacher, walked past them on his way to the assembly. "Time to go in, girls," he urged as he hurried toward the A.V. room.

Miranda took a deep breath and squared her shoulders. "This is it. When I come out of there, I'll have no friends."

"Yes, you will," Lizzie promised. "You'll have me."

Lizzie held out her arm and Miranda linked hers through it. And then the two friends walked into the A.V. room together.

"Okay, everyone," Mr. Escobar said as Lizzie and Miranda slipped into a couple of seats at the rear of the room. "This is the moment we've all been waiting for." The teacher caught himself and nodded to two artsy-looking kids in the front row. "No disrespect to the other finalists from the other schools," he added quickly.

The crowd started to boo and toss wadded-up paper at the other two finalists. It was clear who this group was rooting for.

"Now, now, now, stop," Mr. Escobar said in a voice that sounded like he didn't really care whether it stopped or not. "Let's be nice to our guests."

The crowd threw more trash. Mr. Escobar waited a few seconds before stepping in. "Okay, that's enough," he said finally. "Now, without further ado, 'The Gordo Files,' by David Gordon."

The crowd applauded as the lights went down and the large monitor flickered on at the front of the room.

The huge football player was the first to appear on screen—only Gordo had fuzzed out his face and altered his voice! "Okay, you really want to know my secret?" the voice asked.

"Yeah."

"I'll tell you." The enormous jock pulled out his fuzzy pink rabbit. "Here, pet it."

Lizzie looked around as the audience cracked up. Even the huge football player was laughing. Lizzie grinned, wondering whether he had the fuzzy pink bunny in his backpack.

"Pet it?" the smaller player asked.

The audience laughed some more.

On-screen, the huge football player urged the smaller one to pet the bunny. "I tell you, I do it every time before a game. It'll bring you luck."

The audience whooped and cheered as the film rolled on and the pretty girl in the lunch room let out a long, loud, disgusting burp. Her face had been fuzzed out, too.

The pretty girl giggled as the crowd let out a series of shouts like, "Eww!" and "That's gross!"

Suddenly, a strange voice sounded over the action on the film. "Why don't they just slap a big sign on this school that says 'Loser Farm' and be done with it?"

Those are Miranda's words, Lizzie realized.

Miranda slumped in her seat as the audience went silent. Lizzie cringed, remembering how harsh her friend's tirade had been. Both friends squeezed their eyes shut and sank down in their chairs—they couldn't watch.

"Everyone looks up to the jocks and the cheerleaders," the voice went on, "who are a bunch of stuck-up dirks who are going to end up working the drive-through at Burger Buddy."

A titter ran through the audience.

Wait, Lizzie thought, was that laughter?

Lizzie opened her eyes and peeked at the screen. Miranda's face wasn't on it—just her voice. And it wasn't even *her* voice. Gordo had somehow altered it. Lizzie nudged Miranda, who slowly opened her eyes. On the screen, the guy in the library was busily picking his blurry nose.

"It's this whole place," Miranda's on-screen voice said as the popular crowd continued to embarrass themselves on the video monitor. "It's the way that people say one thing to your face and another behind your back."

"Hey, look," Lizzie whispered. "He just used your voice."

The film cut to an image of kids crowding at the front of the school.

But Miranda's tirade kept on coming. "It's the way the cafeteria serves retired circus animals."

On the monitor, the goulash bubbled away

disgustingly. The crowd cracked up, and let out a chorus of "Ewwws."

Omigosh, Lizzie realized as she looked around, no one is even looking in Miranda's direction. Nobody else even knows it's her voice!

"How did Gordo disguise my voice?" Miranda whispered to her friend. "I mean, it doesn't even sound like me."

"I just get the feeling that nobody's being honest here," the voice went on. "That everybody's afraid to let everybody else know the truth about them."

Kate's image flashed on the screen, alongside her friend and sidekick, Claire. Only you couldn't tell it was them. Like the others, Gordo had blurred their faces and altered their voices.

Lizzie sighed. Hey, at least *I* know who that is up on the screen, she told herself consolingly.

And there was someone else who seemed to know who it was, too. Lizzie looked over at Kate, who was fuming.

"Okay, promise you won't tell anyone?" on-screen Kate asked in a low voice.

"Sure," the video image of Claire promised. "What is it?"

"I'm a year older than everybody," video Kate confessed.

Lizzie grinned. This is my favorite part, she thought, sitting back in her chair.

"You are?" on-screen Claire asked in disbelief.

"Yeah," Kate replied.

"But you're in our grade," Claire said.

"Remember," Kate's image insisted, "you promised not to tell anyone."

"You mean you got held back?" Claire asked.

Video Kate was defensive. "It was only in kindergarten," she said.

"I guess it's not that bad, right?" Claire responded.

"I've been hiding this ever since elementary school," Kate said. "If anybody finds out I'm a year older than everybody else, my whole image will be totally ruined."

The image on the screen froze, and Miranda's altered voice came back on. "Let's face it," the voice said, "it's a school full of fakes." There was a pause, and the voice added, "But it's not so bad, as long as you've got really great friends."

Lizzie peered at the faces around her. Kate looked like she was about to have a fit, but everyone else looked fascinated.

Lizzie grinned. And that, she thought, is what great movies are all about.

Lizzie and Miranda walked up to Gordo after the screening. They didn't even have time to say a word before other kids started hurrying over.

"Yo, dude." Ethan grinned as he walked up to Gordo. "Very cool. But for thirty-five-million couldn't you have blown some stuff up?"

The audience was buzzing as it streamed out of the A.V. room, but one voice sounded over the others, pleading, "Kate, you can't blame me!" Claire trotted after her best friend, looking desperate. "I didn't know we were being taped!"

Kate gave Claire the Hand and glared at Gordo. "A," she said to him nastily, "you'll never eat lunch at this school again. B, whose voice was that?"

"I'm sorry, Kate, I can't reveal that," Gordo said simply. "It's a director's prerogative to keep his sources and his techniques confidential."

Kate snarled at him. "What a dirk," she said, then turned on her heel and stomped away. Claire trailed after her, as usual.

"So, Miranda," Gordo said, "you never told me what you thought of it."

"Well, I know it was supposed to be a big surprise and all, but you could have at least told me so I'd stop stressing and get some sleep," Miranda answered.

"Miranda, I'm your friend," Gordo said simply. "You should know that I've always got your back."

Miranda smiled. "Next time, Gordo, remind me."

"I will," Gordo promised. "So, we're cool?"

Miranda nodded. "Yeah, we're cool."

Lizzie heaved a huge sigh of relief. So we're all cool again. Thank goodness. I should have known that we could trust Gordo, she told herself. On the other hand—Miranda had a point. Why hadn't Gordo just cleared everything up from the beginning?

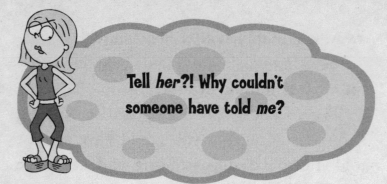

Tell *her*?! Why couldn't someone have told *me*?

"And, Gordo," Lizzie added, "please tell me your days of hidden camera are over."

"They are," Gordo assured her. "It's gotten old school. I'm looking for the next big thing."

i got it! it's a movie about an animated character! She's smart! She's funny! And Brad Pitt is totally in love with her!

Yeah, Lizzie thought, stroking her chin, maybe a story about your average middle-school girl. She's cool, but sometimes maybe a little uncoordinated. And she has two really great friends, Lizzie added mentally as she smiled at Miranda and Gordo. You can't leave out the friends, Lizzie decided. That's definitely the most important part of all.

Don't close the book on Lizzie yet!
Here's a sneak peek at the next
Lizzie McGuire story. . . .

Adapted by Jasmine Jones
Based on the series created by Terri Minsky
Based on a teleplay written by
Nina G. Bargiel & Jeremy J. Bargiel

"**G**reat job, girls," Miss Moran said as she watched Lizzie McGuire and her best friend,

Miranda Sanchez, pack cans of food into cardboard boxes. "This is the most successful food drive Hillridge Junior High has ever had."

"Thanks," Lizzie said brightly, putting another can into the box. "It was actually kind of fun." She had expected the food drive to be sort of boring, but in the end Lizzie had really enjoyed helping out. It made her feel like she was doing something important.

Miranda waggled her eyebrows. "And the extra credit rocks," she said.

"You girls have a knack for this," Miss Moran said. "You know, someone won't go hungry tonight because of all the food you collected. You two might want to think about taking on a *new* volunteer project."

Lizzie looked down at the can of beets in her hand. Someone is going to use these . . . she thought. It was good to know that she was helping people out.

i totally have a knack for this.
i ended world hunger in an
afternoon. Okay, maybe not ended.
But i made a dent!

"Hey, girls!" Mr. McGuire said as he walked into the food collection center carrying a paper bag. Lizzie's mother and annoying little brother trailed behind him.

"Hey," Lizzie said. What's up with the reflecto-dorko gear? Lizzie wondered as she eyed her little brother, who was staring dejectedly at his shoes. Of course, in Lizzie's opinion, Matt was usually dressed like a total dweeb, but today he was over the top—he actually had on a bright orange belt and a sash with a badge on it. Officer Pipsqueak, Lizzie thought.

"Lizzie, you forgot these cans I put out for you." Mr. McGuire handed Lizzie the brown paper sack he had been holding.

Miranda wiped her hands on her jeans. "I gotta go meet my mom. Hasta la bye-bye," she said, giving Lizzie a quick hug and taking off.

"Bye," Lizzie said, smiling as she watched her friend go. Lizzie was glad that she and Miranda were so on the same wavelength. When it came time to do something for the world, Lizzie thought, Miranda and I just tucked up our hair, slapped on our work clothes, and sorted some serious can. And we both loved it! "So," she said, turning to face Matt, "they finally came up with an official uniform for the socially challenged."

"Lizzie!" her parents chorused.

Matt put up a hand and just shook his head sadly. "No, Mom. No, Dad," he said with a sigh. "You can't be mad at her for speaking the truth."

Mrs. McGuire wrapped her hands around Matt's shoulders. "Your brother is wearing his Hall Monitor Safety Patrol Belt," Mrs. McGuire announced.

Wow, Lizzie thought. Mom just said that as though she thinks it's something to be proud of. "Hall monitor?" she repeated, scoffing. "How many garbage cans are you going to get stuck in?"

"See?" Matt whined, turning to his parents. "Even my lame-o sister knows what's coming!"

"Now, honey," Mrs. McGuire said, leaning in closely and giving Matt's shoulder a squeeze, "Hall monitor is a very important job. And you should make the best of it."

"That's right, son," Mr. McGuire agreed, shoving his hands deep in his pockets. "It's a position of honor. I remember when I was a hall monitor. . . ."

Lizzie raised her eyebrows. She'd heard the stories: when her dad was chosen as hall monitor, he had been shoved head-first into a garbage can every day for an entire semester.

Finally, Mr. McGuire had to admit the truth. "Your sister may be right, son."

Lizzie nodded. Sad but true, she thought. Oh, well. At least it's Matt who's going to suffer, and not someone I actually like!

Later that night, Lizzie and Miranda called their best friend David "Gordo" Gordon on three-way calling.

"Gordo, why weren't you at the food drive?" Lizzie asked Gordo.

"I had something more important to do," Gordo said.

"More important than ending world

hunger?" Lizzie snapped. I can't wait to hear this one, Lizzie thought, sitting up straight. He probably spent the afternoon reorganizing his Frank Sinatra records, or watching obscure Japanese art films. Gordo was really sweet and smart, but he could be a little weird sometimes.

"The Science Olympics," Gordo explained. "They're this week. The long-distance paper airplane contest, the egg drop, and the ultimate test of brains and brawn . . . the slow bicycle race."

Bingo, Lizzie thought. Only Gordo would put Egg Drop at the top of his priorities list.

"Uh, Gordo," Miranda said, "Tudgeman always wins those."

Lizzie nodded, even though her friends couldn't see her. Larry Tudgeman was King Nerd of Hillridge Junior High. He'd probably been working on the Science Olympics for twelve months—ever since he won last time.

"Not this year," Gordo shot back. "This year, he's going down."

Lizzie flopped back on her bed. "So, I guess this means you won't be recycling with us," she said.

"Uh," Miranda broke in, "when did we decide on recycling?"

Gee, it almost sounds like Miranda isn't into the idea, Lizzie thought. But that can't be true. It's such an easy thing to do, and it could make such a difference. . . .

"Good luck with that saving the earth thing, guys," Gordo said. "I gotta go drop eggs off the roof." He clicked off.

"Hey, Miranda, meet me at the Digital Bean tomorrow," Lizzie told her best friend. "'Cause we're starting there." Clicking the off button, Lizzie put the phone back in its cradle.

Sorry! That's the end of the sneak
peek for now. But don't go nuclear!
To read the rest, all you have to do
is look for the next title in the
Lizzie McGuire series—